COMBAT
ZONE

COMBAT ZONE

PATRICK JONES

darbycreek

MINNEAPOLIS

The author wishes to thank Susan Olson, Professional Counselor, M.Ed., LPC, for her expertise on military families and thoughtful review of manuscripts in the Support and Defend series, and Judith Klein for her proofreading and copyediting wizardry.

Darby Creek
A division of Lerner Publishing Group, Inc.
241 First Avenue North
Minneapolis, MN 55401 USA

For reading levels and more information, look up this title at
www.lernerbooks.com.

The images in this book are used with the permission of: © Catherine Lane/ E+/Getty Images (teen guy); © iStockphoto.com/CollinsChin (background); © iStockphoto.com/mart_m (dog tags).

Main body text set in Janson Text LT Std 12/17.5.
Typeface provided by Adobe Systems.

Library of Congress Cataloging-in-Publication Data

Jones, Patrick, 1961–
    Combat zone / by Patrick Jones.
      p. cm. — (Support and defend)
    Summary: Justin, a bully at his Pearl Harbor, Hawaii, high school, is confused and angry when his father, a career officer he admires, admits he is gay.
    ISBN 978-1-4677-8053-7 (lb : alk. paper)
    ISBN 978-1-4677-8094-0 (pb : alk. paper)
    ISBN 978-1-4677-8821-2 (eb pdf : alk. paper)
    [1. Fathers and sons—Fiction. 2. Soldiers—Fiction. 3. High schools—Fiction. 4. Schools—Fiction. 5. Coming out (Sexual orientation)—Fiction. 6. Gays—Fiction. 7. Racially-mixed people—Fiction. 8. Pearl Harbor (Hawaii)—Fiction.] I. Title.
PZ7.J7242Com 2015
[Fic]—dc23   2015000596

Manufactured in the United States of America
1 – SB – 7/15/15

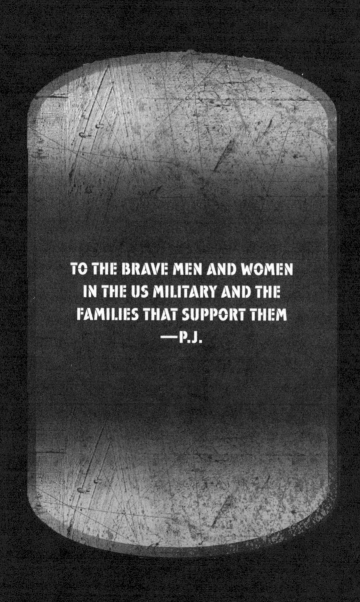

TO THE BRAVE MEN AND WOMEN
IN THE US MILITARY AND THE
FAMILIES THAT SUPPORT THEM
—P.J.

0

"Man up, Justin!" Dad shouts, even though I'm standing next to him. He pats my butt hard and then pushes me into battle, into the combat zone of the mixed martial arts fight in our backyard.

I inhale all the manly scents. Cigar smoke. Steaks on the grill. Embers from the fire pit.

Pounding my chest like a hero from the Greek myths, I inhale the smells in the distance. Jet fuel. Diesel. The aroma of home: Pearl Harbor. Military might in a tropical paradise.

"Go get 'em, Jimmy!" Jimmy Martin's father shouts. He's wasting his words. Jimmy can't take me and everybody knows it, especially Jimmy.

I've already beaten him without throwing a punch, taking a leg, or grabbing a hold. It's not if I beat him, but when. And how badly.

The ref, linebacker superman Mychal's dad, Colonel Stewart, signals for us to start. I adjust my helmet and step forward. We tap gloves and assume our stance. I'd rather go bone on bone, but the dads make us wear MMA gear.

Jimmy circles and throws kicks as the crowd of twenty fathers and sons, all military like my dad, make a human octagon to surround us and cheer. And they're not just military; they're the elite of elite. Navy Seals.

"Come on Jimmy!" a voice shouts. I recognize it and it stings more than the right jab Jimmy lands. It's Calvin Parker, the fourteen-year-old son of Colonel Parker, my dad's best friend. The Parkers moved to Pearl last spring, about the time my parents split up for good. Dad wants Calvin to be my best friend. No way.

After a flurry of punches, Jimmy tries a front kick. I snatch his right leg, trip his left leg, and we're on the grass. I start to pound. Elbows and fists fly as fast as machine gun fire.

"Waste him, Justin!" Mychal yells loud like he does when he's calling the defense on the gridiron.

Jimmy locks his legs around my torso so I've got full mount. Up close, it's a manly fight, but from a distance and to the rednecks of the world, we probably look like two gay dudes doing it. But that's something I wouldn't get caught dead being around.

"Take his back!" Dad yells, as if reading my mind.

As Jimmy bucks like a bronco to escape, I position myself to grab side control. And that's what this is all about anyway: control. Every year before school, Seal sons kick off our private season of MMA fighting to settle old scores and set the hierarchy for the upcoming year so there's no trouble at Pearl High. Of course we've got regular sports at school, but our dads know we need something a little more real.

This establishes who's tough and who's weak. Who rules but also who needs to be protected. At school, we stick together. The Seals are not just a branch of the military; we're a family.

And a family that fights together, stays together. So I stick Jimmy with a hard elbow over the right eye that busts him open. I can't smell the blood, but I can almost taste it in my mouth. Two more quick sharp elbows and it's like I hit red oil as the crimson spurts upward.

Jimmy panics—which is why, unlike me, he'll never make it in the Navy—and that gives me the opening I need. To escape elbows to his face, Jimmy gives me his back. I take his neck.

My right arm slips around his chin, pressed against his throat. With my left parallel to his sweaty and bloody head, I cinch the hold tight. Tighter. Tightest. Rear naked choke. Don't get the wrong idea from the name—there's nothing gay about this fight.

Jimmy quickly taps my arm to signal his surrender. I release the hold and stand in victory.

Jimmy rises, wipes the blood from his brow, and hugs me tight. "Great fight, Justin."

"Get a room, lover boys!" Mychal shouts as Jimmy and me hug. Mychal cackles at his words.

I thank Jimmy for the battle, but he's not my concern. It doesn't matter what he thinks, what Calvin or Mychal think, what anybody thinks except one man: Colonel Edwin Ladd. Dad.

My eyes scan the crowd and it takes a second to find him, just as it took years for us to finally find ourselves in the same home. Same blood, same drive, same warrior heart.

"How did you like that, Colonel Ladd?" I shout over the roar of a jet fighter overhead.

Dad whispers something to Colonel Parker, his buddy, and they laugh. They raise their beer bottles toward me as a sign of respect as I walk, head held high, out of the combat zone as the winner.

2

"Come on, Justin, ten more!" Dad yells as I bench press the heavy metal off my chest.

The weight room at school is better than this makeshift gym in our dank basement—nothing but state of the art for the Spartan athletes of Pearl High. But the weight room's missing one thing: Dad. Given how much he's been in and out of my life, I'd rather spend time here at home than at school's well-lit weight-lifting heaven.

Dad gives so much of himself—for me, for country, for uniform—so I try to give him what he wants. And more. He yells for five reps, I give him ten until it feels like my arms are live grenades with the pin pulled. "That's the way, Justin, that's the way!"

Dad does curls in the corner, not breaking a sweat, but I'm drenched. Moisture drips from my shaved head down onto my workout shorts. I've lived half of my almost eighteen years in Hawaii, yet my body still battles the heat and humidity. "Great fight last night, Justin."

"I feel cheated. It didn't last long enough."

"Now you know how I feel." Dad laughs but that laugh's a fake. While he saw combat in both Iraq and Afghanistan—and has the scars to prove it—Dad's valued more as a trainer and leader. So he's spent most of his career teaching skills, not carrying out missions. I let the comment pass. Dad doesn't talk about the past—either the wars overseas or those stateside with Mom.

"I want you to work with Calvin Parker," Dad says, as he starts curls with his left arm. He'll do fifty reps without taking a deep breath. "Teach him how to fight."

Calvin lasted even less time in his fight with

me than Jimmy did. One punch knockout. The first punch. "That's his dad's job, isn't it?" I ask.

"I taught you self-defense younger than most kids, but those were special circumstances," Dad says. "Larry didn't get a chance to teach Calvin."

I push the bar off my chest like it's on fire. It jars me to hear Dad refer to his fellow officers by their first names. He's Colonel Parker, not Larry. Larry is the name of a limp-wrist civilian who works in a drab office at a computer. Colonel Parker is the name of a warrior.

"Dad, I'm so busy with football, school— just everything."

I wait for him to respond, but there's just the whooshing of the barbell in the windowless basement. He makes the sound I hate most of all: none. Total silence. His greatest weapon.

"It's not my job to teach him fighting." The words "not" and "no" are rare from my lips.

Whoosh. Whoosh. Whoosh.

"Besides he's just a filthy freshman," I say, almost shouting to make up for Dad's silence.

"Why don't I just watch out for him? If anybody picks on him, they'll know I have his back."

Whoosh. Whoosh. Whoosh.

"Nobody's gonna pick on him like I got picked on. He's not different like me."

Clang. The barbell hits the floor. It rolls over toward me, but still no words. When we lived before at Pearl and in California, the fact I looked even the smallest bit different—American dad, Japanese mom—wasn't a big deal. But then in junior high we were stationed in Virginia and it was a different story. Dad taught me how to defend myself. After that, some kids tried me. No redneck pig lover ever insulted me again.

Dad picks up the barbell. "Justin, I'm not asking. It might not be your job, but it is your . . ."

He lets me finish the sentence using the world's most powerful four-letter word. "Duty."

3

"Carpe diem, Justin!" Dad yells out on his way out the side door. He's off to another day at the office—one of the few offices where the job is to teach people how to kill others—while I'm getting ready for the first day of my senior year where I will, as Dad says, seize the day.

Once he's out the door, I text Eric, my best bro. Dad's not a fan of Eric, because he's got no dad and his mom's a drunk, so I keep our friendship on the QT. I confirm the time I'm picking him up. He replies full of four-letter words. He's ying to my yang; red-headed rebel to my Seal son.

I rinse out my bowl and coffee cup and clear the table with military precision. Then I head into my room and check out the closet full of clothes but go straight for one thing. Even though it's not game day, I like to wear my jersey the first day of school, just to remind people who's in and who's out. It's the second-best uniform in the house. Then I realize with Dad gone, I've got a chance to try on the best.

Just like the rest of our house, everything in Dad's bedroom is in perfect order. The sheets are pulled so tight, I could bounce a quarter off the bed and it would hit the ceiling. Deep in his closet, wrapped in plastic, is his dress uniform which is used for special occasions like weddings and funerals.

I carefully remove the hand-pressed uniform and slip the jacket on over my clothes. I'm about an inch shorter than Dad, which I blame on my short Japanese mom. The hat sits on my head, too big, but no matter. According to some teachers at school, my head's too big, but they're just jealous, like most civilians, of what I'll become.

The bright morning light makes the room almost glow as I stand in front of the mirror. Gazing at my reflection, I see myself after the Academy, after my tours of duty, wearing this uniform to my special occasion—my wedding— with my bride-to-be by my side. "Do you, Colonel Ladd . . . ?" I imagine the words. I don't want to be an admiral; I don't want to be a rank lower or higher than my dad. I want to be exactly the same, except unlike Dad, I'll marry right.

* * *

"Looking good, Just Man!" Eric says, as he climbs in the back seat of my red convertible Shelby Mustang. It was my seventeenth birthday present from Dad (who got himself a blue one a few months ago for his fortieth).

Dad never spent a dime on himself—saved everything he earned—until he landed for good on the island. His making light with the green is the surest sign we're staying put. Also he's throwing money at me to cover up the guilt of being gone most of my life.

Mychal, Eric's next door neighbor, leaps in the front seat. If Eric's my yang, then Mychal's my brother from a different mother: mixed race kids with mad football skills run amok.

"So, you got Double D for English?" Eric asks. Mychal laughs so loud he snorts.

"You know it." A bump followed by a laugh. Double D—the estimated bra size of Mrs. Barbara McFadden, Language Arts teacher at Pearl High for the past four years. I thought about failing ninth grade English just to take it over with her. Now, she's teaching AP and I hope I can focus on the books, not just her boobs.

"I'd like to shake those spheres," Eric says. "And tame her shrew."

We all laugh as Eric turns the Shakespeare McFadden teaches into something dirty. "I wonder who will fail the test?" Mychal asks.

"Some homo," I crack. We know anyone who

doesn't check out Double D is definitely gay.

"I wonder sometimes about Jimmy," Mychal adds. "He's a pecker checker, I know that."

That's another test for a guy on your team or in gym class. If he doesn't have his eyes on the shower but instead is looking at places his pupils don't belong, he's gay. Jimmy's got a hot girlfriend, but I think that's just camouflage. "He looks at my junk and I'll choke him out," I say.

"Justin, you gotta be careful," Eric shouts over the music.

"All the anti-bullying bull," Mychal adds. "They should let us sort it out ourselves."

"I'll put the moves on Erin and see if she can handle a real man," I say. Erin Winter is Jimmy Martin's girlfriend but like most girls at Pearl, she could be mine if I wanted her.

"Erin's fine but not as fine as . . ." Eric starts and for the rest of the drive to school, we're off to the races comparing the finer points, profiles, and posteriors of various Pearl High fillies.

4

"Justin, this is the cool of the evening," Dad says as he motions for me to take off my helmet. We're at the peak of Tantalus Mountain, looking down on Honolulu. The lights glow, but the sounds and smells don't make their way this high. In a few hours, the mountain roads won't be trekked by motorcyclists like Dad and me but by stupid drifters who think they're so cool.

I remove my helmet and feel the ocean breeze on my clean-shaven face even at this altitude.

"You played a good game tonight, and that's the cool of the evening," Dad says. "You've done your job. You should enjoy the rewards of your labor, soaking up the world around you."

I wish he'd said great game, but he's right, it was just good. While we won the game easily, I didn't get any sacks and just a few stuffs, but I was double-teamed all night. That was easy for the other team to do since the right tackle next to me, a civilian transfer named Anton, plays too soft. Luckily, I have Mychal behind us, watching our backs and saving our bacon. He's a defensive demon.

"What are you doing this weekend?" Dad asks.

"Don't you mean who am I doing?" Dad doesn't laugh; Mychal would've snorted.

"C'mon, you know being a real man doesn't mean being disrespectful to women." Dad looks at me. I look away—sometimes I forget Dad isn't one of my boys. "Anyway, I thought maybe we'd take a long ride on Sunday," he says, letting it go.

"Just us?"

"I thought maybe Larry and his son Calvin could come with us," Dad says.

"He's too young to drive," I remind Dad. I

remind myself to ask Calvin what he thought about his freshman English teacher, Mrs. McFadden. See if he passes the gay test.

"We'll make it work." I don't say anything because I've heard that before from Dad, and I think it's the only time he's ever lied to me. When I was little, I'd ask him about him and Mom since they almost never got along, and he'd say, "We'll make it work." It never did, but what can you expect when half of a machine is made of strong metal and the rest of weak fiber.

"Do you miss Mom?" I ask Dad. I noticed he's staring not down at the city, but far off, over the ocean, toward Japan. After the divorce and he got custody, Mom moved back home.

Dad's silent again. Is he punishing me for asking? Or doesn't he have an answer?

I start to talk again, but he puts his helmet on and motions for me to do the same. He revs the mighty engine of the Harley; I respond in kind. Dad zips up his jacket and gives me a thumbs-up sign. I do the same and now we're off, seeing who can be first down the mountain. He wins, but only because I let him. The turns are sharp and scary, and adrenaline pumps through my body like it does when I'm fighting, wrestling, or crushing some helpless quarterback who's trying to make a pass.

As we cruise down the hill, the cool of the evening gives way to the warmth of the gray pavement and body heat of a million-plus people crammed on this little island. But it could be worse. I could be back in Virginia— or worse yet, in Japan with my mom. All the way down the mountain, we talk to each other about nothing much, using the Bluetooth headsets clipped under our helmets.

At the bottom of the mountain, Dad pulls off to the side of the road. I fall in line just a few seconds behind. He takes off his helmet, and the setting sun seems to bounce off his crew cut. My helmet stays on but I cut the engine so I can hear. "So, Sunday with Larry and Calvin."

It's no longer a question but a statement. An order. And all orders are to be obeyed.

Dad pulls out his phone and makes a call. I use the time to text Eric.

It's late, but there's got to be a party someplace (although as Eric always says, "Just Man, where we are, that's where the party is"). Eric answers with an address I don't know. I'm tired, so I'm having second thoughts until I see three words "Erin Drunk Hurry" flash on my phone.

The cool of the evening is about to heat up.

5

"Just Man, glad you made it!" Eric smacks my back as his welcome-to-the-party gesture.

"Is Jimmy with her?" I ask, looking around the crowded party for Erin.

"He's here, but staying mostly in the basement playing quarters," Eric slurs. He offers me a red cup full of something, but he should know better. I follow the athlete's code of honor to the letter. Looking around I see fellow players, like Anton and Mychal, ignoring it. Mychal's hero enough to get away with it, but Anton's game isn't at immunity level. He'd better watch himself or else.

"Where is Erin?" I see other fine females of various shapes, sizes, and colors.

Eric points toward a crowded screened-in back porch. It's only ten feet away, but I could use a couple of blockers to get through the packed room. I'm almost there when this junior semi-hot girl, Allison Sanders, steps in front of me, drink in hand, and my name on her lips.

"Justin, what are you doing here?" she whispers in my ear. I smell whiskey on her breath.

"Just looking for a friend," I answer as she latches onto my arm. She wears gold rings on every finger, four blue bracelets on both wrists, and a silver stud in her nose. "I gotta go."

"But you just got here." She pretends to pout with lips as red and ripe as cherries.

"Like I said, I'm looking for a friend."

She wraps her arm around my neck, pulls me closer. "I could be your friend, Justin."

I don't push her away. She's fine, but there's something about Erin, maybe because she'd be hard to get. I'd be doing her a favor if Jimmy can't man up. "Maybe later, Allison."

"You should call me." When she reaches for her cell, she spills her drink on my chucks.

"What's wrong with you?" I hear Anton's voice from behind. I turn around. There stands Anton with Mychal and some of the other black players on the team. "She's drunk. That's sad."

"All the girls go for me, drunk or sober," I spit back at him.

"I was . . ." Allison starts, but Anton steps in front of her. She takes the hint and leaves.

"We shouldn't be at this party," Anton mumbles. I shrug and start again for Erin on the porch. "I messed up big time. We could get in trouble with Coach. We should bounce. You got a ride?"

"Look, I'm here to . . ." I start but stop speaking when I see Jimmy is now by Erin's side. Ding, ding, ding, game over.

"I don't trust these people. They're not family, like us," Anton says. I don't correct him. A football team isn't a family; it's a bunch of people wearing the same uniform. The Seals are family—bound not by name or uniform, but tradition, honor, and duty. Words a civilian like Anton couldn't understand.

"Can I talk to you about something, Justin?" Anton's pushy, like lots of transfer kids, trying too hard. Since we share the defensive line, he seems to think that we should be best buddies. He's broken off from the group as Mychal and the others leave to look for more wine, women, or both.

I pull a Dad and answer by saying nothing, turning my back, and heading for the door. I've lost my appetite for going after Erin. Like a shadow, Anton's behind me. I pick up the pace and I hear his heavy footsteps follow. When I get to my car, he's standing there a little out of breath, looking like a lost puppy.

"Can you give me a ride home?" Anton asks. He's got the same tone Allison had.

"No." I shut him down like he was a halfback thinking he could get around me on the outside.

"Please, Justin," Anton says in such a little voice coming from a big guy. I start to say no again, then I think about all the times I was the new kid in school and got treated like crap until I showed them who I was. But Anton hasn't got the same drive. That's another casualty of a civilian childhood: you take life for granted rather than as a life-or-death proposition. "Please."

I text Eric and Mychal, tell them I'm leaving and motion for Anton to get in the car. He's like a little kid at Christmas in the Shelby. "I owe you," he says, all nervous.

"Don't worry about it." I turn the key, put it into drive, and push the metal to the floor.

"There's something I need to tell everyone on the team. Since the guys kinda look up to you, I thought you'd be a good person to come out to first," Anton blurts out. "Especially since your—"

I screech the car to a halt. He's still trying to talk, but he can't finish the sentence. That's hard to do with my fist rearranging his facial features.

6

"Justin, you're grounded," Dad says as we walk from the principal's office to our cars. He walks two feet in front of me like he doesn't want to be seen with me or something.

"Dad, wait up!" I shout after him, but he doesn't turn around, so I pick up the pace.

"I didn't do anything!" I protest.

He opens his car door, not taking the bait.

"It's not my fault!" When I'm wrong I can man up, but I'm right. We both got to know it.

"You broke Anton's jaw," Dad says through clenched teeth, sounding like his own jaw was shattered. "You're lucky he isn't pressing charges."

"I was defending myself. And I did drop him off at home." I repeat the same thing I told him, the principal, and Coach Young. "He came on to me. I don't want some messed up freak—"

"Enough!" Dad shouts so loud and hard it feels like a punch to my face.

"You taught me to defend myself," I remind him.

He narrows his eyes like a wild animal about to strike. "So you wouldn't be bullied."

"I don't see how this is any different, some filthy—"

"Enough!"

Dad and I stare at each other just the way I lock eyes with the guard across from me on the line, the wrestler across from me on the mat, or the son-of-a-Seal fighter that I'm battling for turf. He blinks, so I man up and apologize. "Look, I'm sorry. I'll tell Anton that. I overreacted. You're angry."

Now Dad won't look at me. He studies the school parking lot pavement like a Seal would memorize a map before a mission. "I'm not angry at you, Justin. I'm just . . ."

I know what's coming. Maybe if I say it, then it won't sting as much. "Disappointed."

"No, I'm ashamed of you." He turns his back and opens the car door. My knees melt in the heat, and the screech of his tires driving away feels like a bandage ripped off a fresh wound. If only he knew that I'd done it for him.

* * *

By practice, everybody's heard about me punching out Anton. I don't tell them the truth like I did Dad, so I tell them a story about the two of us fighting over Allison. Everybody buys it.

Coach Young puts us through a hard practice, punishing everyone with his anger at me for forcing him to find a new right tackle. Coach said he'd let this pass, but that I'd better not screw up again or I'm gone.

Some guys hit the weight room after practice, but I'll save my lifting for home—maybe Dad will be cooled off by then. I guess he expects, no matter what the circumstances, for me to display discipline, but I wonder what he would've done if some gay freak came on to him. After I shower, I head toward the Shelby. I'm about to text Eric when I hear Mychal call my name.

I stop and face Mychal. He's smaller, faster, and almost as popular as me. He's one of these guys, like Dad, when he walks in a room, everybody stops and wants his attention, his approval.

"So that whole thing you said about Allison, that's BS," Mychal says. "Anton's gay, right, so something else happened . . ."

Mychal's my best friend on the team and a Seal son, so I tell him how Anton came on to me and I had to defend myself. He thinks it's funny that the reason I was at the party was to hit on Erin, and then I ended up getting hit on. I fail to find the humor in any of it until he starts talking about fixing up Anton and Jimmy. "That frees up Erin from Jimmy and gets Anton out of your hair, or pants, or wherever."

He puts the bad mouth on Anton for a long time until it's time for me to bounce. I like hanging with my friends, but I never miss dinner with Dad. It's a ritual and a rule.

When I get home, I see Dad's car is gone; either he's working late or hanging out with his buddies. There's a bucket of chicken on the table. It's still warm, so he just left like he wanted to avoid eating dinner with me. Next to the food is a note. I wonder if it's another slap to the face.

But it's worse. It's a kick below the belt. It says, "It's your mother's birthday. Call her."

I salute the note from Colonel Ladd before I crumple it up and toss it in the empty trash.

7

"Justin, you look so handsome," Mom gushes. As always, we're on Skype, which I grew to know very well during Dad's various deployments. When I was a kid, Dad seemed like a character on a TV show. I saw him more on a grainy screen than in the flesh.

I grunt, fake a smile, and try not to roll my eyes. Every conversation with Mom since the divorce, Dad getting custody, and her moving back to Japan has been the same. There's a huge distance between us, which would be true even if she was living next door rather than across the ocean.

"So how is your senior year?" Mom asks. "You must be so excited."

That's so Mom, trying to tell me how I should feel. Like when Dad was deployed, she'd try to do all this crap to get me to connect to my feelings. I was trying to be strong for Dad, but she was making me weak, like her. "I'm ready for it to be over and get into the Academy."

The Naval Academy in Annapolis. Dad wants it as bad as me, sometimes more. He came up the hard way, joining the service at eighteen and working his way up the ranks. I'd do it his way, but his mind is set on this. There's no denying the desires of Colonel Edwin Ladd.

"I do wish you'd reconsider that, Justin," Mom says in that hypercritical tone. "The Navy life is—well, look at what it did to our family."

I want to say *my family is fine because you're not part of it*, but I don't. There's a burning rage of anger at her that I can't control or understand. I used to think Dad left home all the time to get away from her. I thought he'd rather die in some lonely desert than live with Mom.

I pull a Dad and leave her twisting slowly in the silence, before I say. "I can't."

She pauses, sips some tea, and paints on another smile. "How is your father?"

Mom and I talk maybe once a month because Dad insists, but he's certainly not setting an example in this area. As far as I know, they've not spoken for a while. I'm not sure what, if anything, to tell her since his life is none of her concern, but if I talk about Dad, then I don't have to talk about me. "He likes being back at Pearl. He has lots of friends."

"Men do gravitate toward your father," she says. "He's got a presence, I admit. I remember the first time I saw him." And she's telling me this story again, but her version, which is all romantic. Dad's version is simpler, with a lesson: "I was young and stupid. She was a mistake but you were not, so I tried to make it work for your sake, son. Don't be stupid like me."

As Mom talks, I hope she doesn't notice me texting Eric to set up a time to work on some AP English, but he's not answering. I hit up Mychal and a few teammates until I get some guys to say they'll come to my house. I need help with my grades; I need a reason to get off this call.

"Mom, sorry, I've got to get to some homework," I say, all truthful. Now.

"I understand."

"So, happy birthday. I'm sorry I forgot to say it when we first talked."

She smiles, the fakest one yet. "That's okay, Justin. I'm just glad you called."

I don't tell her Dad made me call and had to remind me in the first place. "Maybe I'll come over there during winter break if I don't have wrestling meets," I say, knowing full well we always have a holiday wrestling tournament. I doubt she recalls that, so it seems like a real offer.

"I'd like that," she says. "I miss you, Justin. Be careful."

"I always wear a helmet for combat sports," I joke, but she doesn't laugh.

"No, listen, Justin, be careful now that it's just you and your father. He is . . ."

And she pauses, or maybe the screen freezes, so I finish it. "He is a great man."

"He's a good man." Her fake smiles vanishes. "But he's not the man you think he is."

"What do you mean by that?" I shout at the screen, but she's hung up. There's no longer an image of my mom on the computer, but a blank screen, a black mirror reflecting my hurt face.

8

"Justin, this is so cool," Calvin Parker says, all excited and immature like the kid brother I never had or wanted. He rode up Tantalus Mountain on the back of his dad's machine but then down with Dad. He got back on his dad's Harley for the rest of the ride to the north shore.

"It's a great way to spend a Sunday." I wonder if freshmen understand senior sarcasm. I have so much to do, and yapping with Calvin isn't on the list. Even being grounded because of Anton, except for school, practice, and trips with Dad, I'm falling behind in my classes. But worse, I've been too busy to find someone to invite to the

Homecoming dance. Erin? Allison? Who?

"How long have you guys been riding your bikes?" Calvin asks. The two of us sit at a rest stop bench under a hot midday sun. Surfers, swimmers, and skydivers frolic on the beach behind us.

I wish Dad and Colonel Parker would return from wherever they took off to so I could get back home and away from this human mosquito buzzing in my ear. I don't let my thoughts go any further in that direction. "Two years."

"I can't wait to get my license so Dad and I can ride up here together like you guys."

"Calvin, who knows if you'll even be here in two years," I say, shutting him down. "You know how many places I've lived in eighteen years? Ten, and this is my third time living in Hawaii, except this time with the wars done overseas, we're staying. We've not bugged out in four and that's a record."

"That's what my dad says too," Calvin says. "You like it here?"

"No, I don't like it here, I love it," I say, trying not to smile. "I mean, not only is it a paradise, you got your Seal family all around you. Sun. Sand. Beaches."

"Bikinis," he says and then giggles.

"How do you like Mrs. McFadden?" I ask. More giggles.

"I'd like to see her in a bikini."

"Or less." I add. He laughs like a man rather than giggling like a girl this time.

"Are you going to teach me to fight?" he asks. I sip from a water bottle. He does the same as we wait for our fathers to return. "Do you know karate, kung-fu, judo, maybe ju-jitsu?"

"Why, because I'm part Asian?" I snap. "Do you want me to make you sushi, too?"

"No, Justin, sorry, nothing like that," he says, sounding scared.

"Well, if you want to be a good fighter, stop backing down," I tell him. "If you're the aggressor, then the other person has to fight your fight. What are you good at? Kicks? Throws?"

"Mostly getting knocked out, but that's not much of a skill." He laughs again. I join in.

"You have to learn how to take a strike, but also how to use someone's striking ability to your advantage," I say. "Fighting is just like chess but it's way faster and with more blood."

"Except you're a king and I'm a pawn."

"Well, maybe I can get you to bishop level."

"Great, then I can only move diagonally."

I laugh again. This kid's actually pretty funny.

"My dad taught me how to defend myself when I was young so I had a heads-up on these guys," I say. "With some practice, you'll be tough as nails."

"Thanks, Justin," he says. "I really want to fit in since we're staying here for good."

"So, why do you think that you guys are taking root?" I sip the cool water, lean back on the bench, and soak in the sun. I wait but Calvin doesn't answer. "You hear me, Calvin?"

Calvin mumbles something. I sit up straight and stare at him. He's blushing. "Yeah."

"So, why didn't you answer me?" I ask. "Why do you think that you're staying . . ."

"You know, Justin," Calvin says softly.

"Know what? The sun's messing with you. How would I know anything about your dad?"

He leans in toward me and whispers, "You know about *our* dads."

Just as I'm pulling back to hit him, Dad and Colonel Parker ride up. Before they can get their helmets off, I've taken off on my bike.

9

"Justin, slow down," Dad's voice screams right in my ears, thanks to the Bluetooth.

For eighteen years I've done whatever he asked, whenever he asked. I speed up on the Harley, even as I come to a sharp turn to turn off the main road, heading back toward Pearl.

They've got Calvin on the back of one of their bikes so they'll have to go slower. And I guess they just can't separate from each other. I keep expecting Dad to pull up behind me but I've got a good head start now.

I drive straight for the house. I consider riding the Harley until it runs out of gas or I run out of road, which I guess is the worst part about living on island: there's a limit to how far you can go.

"I want to talk to you," Dad says in my ear. I pull the bike into the driveway, tear off my helmet, and hurl the Bluetooth against the garage. It breaks in half. I get off the bike, kick the stand, and race toward the broken device. I stomp on the two pieces with the black heel of my riding boot like they're cockroaches on the floor, and then I grind the smashed pieces into smaller pieces until they resemble electronic sawdust.

I head inside the house and race toward my room. Like I was packing for an overnight wrestling camp, I grab my gym bag out of the closet and start throwing in clothes. I put my phone on speaker and call Eric. For once, he answers instead of waiting for a text.

"Eric, I need a place to stay." Mychal's dad would return me to his Seal brother.

"Just Man, what's going on?"

"I can't say," I answer. I won't say because it

isn't true. Calvin's just a stupid kid who doesn't know anything about anything except how to get under my skin.

"I'll ask the momster."

"I'm coming over anyway," I answer. He starts asking more questions, but I'm not answering because none of this nonsense is anyone's business. "I'll be there in fifteen."

As I'm hanging up with Eric, Dad's calling. I turn my phone off. I pack my charger and football jersey. I figure I can survive a few days until I can work out what I'm going to do and where I'm going to live. Or maybe Eric's mom will be too drunk to notice I'm there.

On the way out of the house, I start to detour into Dad's bedroom to take one last look, but the thought of it gags me. Instead, I head down to the weight room and pick up a twenty pound dumbbell. This 180 pound idiot needs twenty more pounds of stupid.

I open the garage and see our matching Shelby Mustangs. I throw my stuff—other than the dumbbell—in my trunk, put down the roof, turn the music up, and drive out of the garage. With the car in park, I head back to the garage, dumbbell in hand.

Six feet from Dad's car, I hurl it at the windshield. The glass explodes onto the garage floor. I watch it break into a thousand pieces. Like my life.

I take a moment to savor the result of my rage before I turn back toward my car.

But at the bottom of the driveway—Dad. The bike blocks one side of the driveway; he blocks the other. His helmet hangs in his left hand, his phone in his right. He says nothing.

I look back at the shattered glass and then try to stare at Dad, but I can't. I've seen him through grainy screens from across thousands of miles while gunfire could be heard in the distance. I've heard him through the snap, crackle, and pop of bad telephone connections. I've watched videos he made and posted for me. All those years and miles away, we stayed connected. He remained my friend, my mentor, my hero, my inspiration, my father, my future.

Until today. Now he's just a stranger I used to know.

"Justin, what is wrong with you?!" the man at the bottom of the driveway yells. I don't answer because a man I once respected told me to never talk to strangers. I jump back in the car, turn the wheel hard to the right, hit the gas, and exit across the once-perfect front lawn.

10

"Justin, they need to see you in the office," Mrs. McFadden says. She says it loud enough for others to hear. Like a zombie, I rise from my chair, not even bothering to check her out, and start for the door. It seems like "Do as you're told" is programmed deep within my DNA.

"What up?" Eric and Mychal call out.

"I don't know," I reply, trying to figure out what I've done to get me into trouble. Mychal, Eric, and I were late this morning. Staying up all night playing *Call of Duty* will cause that, but that's nothing. Seal-son football players in this school get away with most anything. If I had been a civilian and punched out Anton, I'd be in juvie or at least serving a suspension.

"If you're not back in fifteen, I'll send in reinforcements," Mychal cracks. I'd laugh if it was funny or if anything was funny, but despite the bright sun, there's nothing but dark clouds for me today.

As I walk down the hall toward the office, I consider sprinting the other way, but fight the urge because I need school, especially football. I need a team, a unit, a family.

Once inside the principal's outer office, "I was told to see . . ." is as far as I get. Her secretary sits at her desk, but she's not alone in the room. In front of the door is a uniformed military police officer and next to him is Colonel Edwin Ladd, United States Navy.

"Justin, you're coming home," Colonel Ladd announces.

I say nothing, so he whispers something to the secretary. She finds a reason to exit.

"Justin, listen to me. You're coming home

with me, right now," Colonel Ladd says, his voice louder, maybe about a five on a scale of one to ten. I've heard his ten, I've taken it. Bring it on. "We need to talk. You can come home with me or I can have Officer Jenkins escort you to the brig."

His arms are crossed over his chest; I let mine dangle at my sides. My feet don't move.

"Justin, I'm giving you a choice."

I stare at Colonel Ladd but turn toward the officer. "What did I do?"

"Property damage on a military facility," the MP answers.

"But I'm not in the military, so you can't do anything," I spit back.

"Justin, you're not making this easy," the man with the ribbons on his chest says.

"And I'm never going to be in the military. Ever."

"We can transfer you to civilian authorities for prosecution of sentence," the MP says with the tone of a finely tuned robot, also known as a good soldier, a flesh and bone drone.

I step toward the officer, staring at him and put my hands out in front of me. "Do it."

"Justin, think about this," Colonel Ladd says. "You'll lose everything. Your spot on the team. Your chance at the Academy. I don't know what's wrong with you, but whatever it is . . ."

"You."

"What are you saying?" The volume drops to three.

"You." My hands remain in front of me waiting for the cuffs, but the cuffs remain on the MP's belt. "You're what's wrong."

"Justin, you can't keep this up."

I think of all the things I could say, but they would only embarrass me more. "I'm going back to class." I put my hands in my pockets while Colonel Ladd and the MP stare at each other.

"Justin, please come home." The volume drops almost to one. A whisper.

"No."

Colonel Ladd motions for the MP to stand

next him. Whispers are exchanged. More secrets to be kept from me. Colonel Ladd has quite the experience and expertise in this area.

The MP takes the cuffs off his belt and motions for me to turn around. I do as I'm told.

"Put him in the back seat of my car," Colonel Ladd commands. "He's going home."

OO

"Justin, you two finish up," Colonel Ladd shouts from the kitchen window. "Dinner's in five." Colonel Parker is in the kitchen with him.

Like I've done since I was brought home against my will this afternoon, I say nothing. I guess Dad thought Colonel Parker and Calvin would get me out of my funk. Great idea.

"So, takedowns, how do you do that?" Calvin asks. I wasn't going to have anything to do with him, but he reminded me I said I'd show him fighting stuff. Fine. If that's what he wants, who am I to resist his invitation?

"Listen, the way to learn anything is to do

it, so stand up." He follows orders. He'll make a good soldier—if he can learn to live with pain.

He no sooner assumes what looks like a fighting stance than I shoot. I grab him around both legs, lift him in the air, and slam him hard against the grass. Even as we're going down, I twist my body so when we land, I'll have side control. He groans when he hits the grass and has the air knocked out of his body; it was his turn to know what that felt like. "That's a receipt," I hiss.

"What did I do to . . . ?" he starts to ask me, but I cut off his wind easily. I lace my arms together and have him locked in a rear naked choke. I apply enough pressure to make it hurt, but not so much that he'll black out. Enough so he'll talk, but not so much that he can scream.

"Why did you lie to me?"

"Lie?"

"What you said about your father and my dad." I crank my right arm tighter.

"You're hurting me."

I got my mouth against his right ear. "That's

the idea. Now you know how I felt."

"It's not a lie," he croaks. With the pressure against his throat he's barely able to talk.

"It is a lie. My dad's not gay."

"Justin, let me go."

"I should twist your lying head off."

"Did you talk to him?"

I wrap my legs around his twisting torso and squeeze there. "This is what it feels like to have your life crushed."

"I'm sorry, Justin. They said you knew," Calvin says, although now it's through tears.

"There's nothing to know."

"I'm sorry. Forget it."

"You forget you told me," I tell him. "If you tell anyone else, I'll rip your head off."

"Let me go."

I squeeze my legs tighter; he's as good as paralyzed. "It never . . ."

"Justin, what are you doing?" Colonel Parker yells from a distance. I let his son go. Calvin starts coughing and wheezing but quickly covers his face to hide the tears.

"I was teaching him how to fight," I yell over my shoulder. "I thought that's what you wanted."

I'm still on the ground, so he's towering over me. With his Seal training, he could kill me twenty different ways in less than ten seconds. "That's not what it looked like."

I stare up at Colonel Parker. "Lot of things are like that."

"Like what?"

"Not what they look like," I answer, and then turn to the kid. "Know what I mean, Calvin?"

Through the coughing, he manages to answer. "Sure thing, Justin."

"Well, next time go easy; he's just learning." Colonel Parker smiles and offers me a hand. I want to kick him between the legs. I wave away his help; I don't want him touching me.

"I've got to learn," Calvin says as he rises. He wipes the grass stains from his jeans with his left hand, while with his right, he tries to cover up the other stain: I made him wet his pants.

12

"Justin, I'm not interested," Erin says. I got one arm over the top of her head, resting over her locker, the other on her right side. If it was MMA, I'd squeeze and she'd tap, but so far, she's not surrendering. "I'm already going to Homecoming with Jimmy. You know that."

"I heard he's taking somebody else," I whisper like some big secret.

"Whoever told you that is lying."

"Got the truth straight from the horse's mouth," I lie.

"I don't believe you. Jimmy wouldn't even look at another girl."

I laugh. "Who said he's taking a girl? Mychal said he's taking Anton Washington."

She gets this look on her face like she just stubbed her toe. Hard.

"I thought you knew about Jimmy," I press forward like I'm rushing the passer. "I mean everybody on the team knows. He's always checking us out. And Anton's a sure thing."

She bites her bottom lip. I'm not going to tell her about Anton coming on to me. "If you're saying this to make me mad," she says in quivering voice, "you're doing a good job."

I take another step closer, drop the arm so it's almost resting on her shoulder. "I like you, Erin, and it makes me sad to know you'll be all alone in your house on Homecoming night while Jimmy and Anton are doing whatever it is disgusting freaks like them do. So, come with me. You've probably heard I'm a better fighter than Jimmy, and trust me, Erin, that's not the only thing I can do better than him."

She slaps me hard on the cheek, pushes past

me, and walks away. "So, that's a maybe," I yell after her, but she's running, no doubt to find Jimmy to defend her. Thank you very much.

* * *

"Hey, Allison. Mind if I sit down?" I ask. I haven't seen her since the post-game party and I don't know her that well, except that she came on to me. She's at a table with a small group, and a couple of her friends start whispering.

"Not at all, Justin," she responds. The girls eat salads for lunch. I got a backpack full of power bars.

"You all going to the Homecoming game?" I ask them. Everybody nods. "We're gonna crush those guys. It's gonna be a war. The line is going to a combat zone. You watch for me, number 99. I'll be right in the mix. Any of you have boyfriends on the team?"

For some reason this generates a slew of whispers, giggles, and embarrassed looks, but none of them say anything except a bland blonde with long hair. "My boyfriend is in band."

I poke Allison under the table. When she looks over at me, I roll my eyes. She laughs.

"How about the Homecoming dance?" My question evokes the same responses. "Any of you hear that Jimmy Martin and Anton Washington are going together? Gross, right?"

Lots of nervous laughter, sipping of sodas, and crunching of salads to cover that none of them know how to respond. Of course, the second that they can, they'll spread the news via text and Twitter.

"Maybe Allison and I can get some photos of them."

"You're taking Allison?" bland blonde asks. Allison's face is seven shades of blush.

"Of course. Didn't she tell you?" I say and then put my arm around Allison's shoulders. She doesn't try to pull away; she moves a little closer. "Allison, why didn't you tell them?" Allison stumbles for an answer. "There's only one thing wrong; I think Allison should've been Homecoming Queen, don't all of you?" More nods and smiles. I'm laying it on thicker than syrup over pancakes. "Too bad the school decided to have two queens this year."

"Two?" Allison asks.

I answer. "Yeah, two queens: Anton and Jimmy."

13

"Justin, you ready?" Colonel Stewart asks. I nod and bang my gloves together. Jimmy responds the same, although I don't sense he's hiding a smile behind his mouthpiece like I am.

"Then get it on!" Stewart yells over the shouting Seal fathers and sons. Most everyone has already watched one battle tonight as we eked out a last-minute victory over East High. As predicted, it was a war on the scrimmage line, but Mychal played a stellar game. His normal.

But football can't always scratch the itch, so I'm glad for the chance for a quick real fight in the backyard while the girls go get prettied up for the dance.

"Get him, Jimmy! Don't back down!" Colonel Martin shouts. I hear no encouragement from Colonel Ladd, which is fine with me. Our almost week-long battle of silence remains locked in a stalemate. He didn't wish me luck before the game, which is fine since I don't need his encouragement. Or support. Or love. Or anything. All I need is an exit strategy.

Jimmy plays tight end, so he didn't put as many minutes on the field as I did, but he did take a hellacious hit catching the winning touchdown pass. Maybe he thinks he's a superhero, which is why he challenged me to a fight after Erin blathered to him like a baby.

"Come on, Justin!" Calvin yells out. He was against me last time. I'd prefer that.

Jimmy's throwing bombs from the get-go, trying to take my head off, but I duck most of them or sidestep. He tries a few kicks, but again he misses more than he hits.

"Fight, Justin!" somebody yells, maybe Calvin. Somebody who doesn't understand fighting or war. It's not about the first punch or the last, but the right strike at the right time.

Jimmy shoots, which I block. He should know better, since my winter sport is wrestling while his is basketball. He can a hit a three, but no way is he getting a double leg on me.

"Jimmy, let's go!" His dad is loud. Basic training drill instructor loud.

When Jimmy tries to rush for another takedown, I underhook his arms with mine. Rather than tossing him to the ground with a judo throw, which I could easily do, I force my arms so I get my hands locked behind his head. I pull down on his head while bringing my knee toward his face. It's a basic MMA equation: face meets knee equals lights out.

Except, as I bring my right knee up, he snatches it and pushes me to the grass. He lands on top of me, but doesn't have the skill to get full mount or even side control. I easily escape, but as I get back up, I realize it's a mistake. On the ground, I own him. When we stand again, he hits two quick right jabs, one right between my eyes. I don't see stars; I see an opportunity.

Playtime is over. Scissors beats paper, and he's about to get his head chopped off.

I throw fists, but it's the knee I'm looking to use, as bait. When there's an opening, he reaches for my leg, grabs it, and forces me to the ground. He tries to throw punches but most of them miss. So intent on knocking me out, he leaves himself open. When Jimmy leans toward me to drop a hammer fist, I snatch his neck and wrap him up like a Christmas present in a guillotine choke. With his head encircled, he can't move anything but his eyelids. He taps my leg.

And I apply more pressure. He taps harder, but it's dark so I wonder if anyone notices his black glove frantically smacking against my black trunks. I like Jimmy and he's got guts to want to fight me, but this isn't about him. Too bad he doesn't know that. In a few seconds, he won't know anything as I put him to sleep. Goodnight moon. Goodnight Jimmy.

"Let him go!" shouts a most unwelcome voice. Colonel Edwin Ladd, US Homosexual.

I clench tighter, trying to pull Jimmy's head off and stuff it down the Colonel's throat.

"Now!" Colonel Ladd pries my hands from Jimmy's neck. I stand, but Jimmy stays down.

"Get your filthy hands off me!"

"You watch your mouth!" Colonel Ladd yells. Seal fathers and sons know something's up. Pretty soon, there's a bunch of them standing between Colonel Ladd and me. The veins on both of our necks are taut like blue cables and neither of us blinks. To be continued.

14

"Justin, I need to get home," Allison says. We've left the Homecoming dance, which Jimmy attended with Erin, not Anton. We're just driving around, top down and music up. Mychal told me about a party, but I don't need to be around other guys, I need to be one.

"Why?"

"Because my dad said he wanted me home by midnight," she says. Colonel Ladd said the same to me in one of those "man to man" moments at the door, except he's not a real man.

"Your dad's a civilian, right? So his words can't carry that much weight," I say and turn the music louder. Before, I would've said, "He's not a Seal like my father."

She turns the music down, moves closer, trying to make nice like she did at the dance. "I saw you talking to Jimmy. What was that about?"

Like Fight Club, what happens at Seal sons' fight night stays there. Nobody talks.

"Nothing," I tell her. "I apologized for going off on him and talking smack. He didn't like it, but he accepted it because it's not like he has any choice in the matter."

"You shouldn't spread rumors," Allison says. I laugh at some girl saying that.

"You're right," I concede. "Especially a terrible one about somebody being gay."

"It's fine if Jimmy or Anton are gay," Allison says. "And it shouldn't be terrible to even say something like that about someone, but that's the world we live in."

"Maybe the world you live in." I press a little harder on the gas. "In my world, that's not a real man. In my world, in the world of the Seals, that's not what being a man is about."

She lets go my arm and inches away from me. "They got rid of that stupid policy for the military, and gay people can marry in Hawaii. It's not about being a man; it's about personal freedom."

"I hope you don't actually believe anything you're saying," I counter. I push the gas harder now. My midnight moonlight drive turned dark in a hurry.

"Justin, I thought you were smart, but you're saying a bunch of stupid stuff, so just take me home." She's on the other side of the car. She rolls up the window and rests her head against it.

"Maybe you're a lesbo freak and that's why you're saying this?" I slow the car.

"And the words you use. They are so offensive," Allison says. "I thought you were like this smart athlete, really cool. I always had a crush on you, but you're not cool or smart at all."

"Want to prove it?" I turn into an empty parking lot.

"Prove what?"

"That you're not gay."

She pulls out her phone. "I'm calling my father."

"No, Allison, you're not." I snatch the phone from her hand. She reaches for it but I've got it in my grip. She starts to shout at me but shuts up when I put the phone in my pants.

"That's not funny, Justin!"

"Prove me wrong." I turn the phone off. "You want your phone, reach for it."

And we sit in that parking lot for an hour, not moving. The only sound is my phone ringing.

Another stalemate, except there's no way of settling it that ends well for me. I know I'm embarrassing myself. I can't keep going like this, but I don't know how to stop.

Finally she breaks the silence. "Justin, this was a mistake for both of us. Just take me home."

Having no exit strategy, this seems like a way out. When I pull in the driveway of her house, all the lights are on. Mine's not the only Shelby Mustang in the driveway: there's a blue one with a recently replaced windshield. Allison's parents and Colonel Ladd emerge from the front door. Allison starts from the car, but I pull her back and make sure that Colonel Ladd observes me planting a quick but full kiss on Allison's lips seconds before she slaps my face.

15

"Justin, what is your deal?" Eric asks. We're outside his house at two in the morning. I peeled out from Allison's before Colonel Ladd could get close to me. I couldn't think of where to go except Eric's.

"Up for some *Call of Duty*?" I ask.

"Go home," Eric says through a yawn. He doesn't ask about Homecoming, mainly because he thinks all that stuff is a joke, which is what I like about him. As a Seal son, I'm expected to follow the rules and fit in, but Eric just doesn't care. He's the courageous one.

"Et tu, Brute?" I toss Shakespeare his way as

if to prove Allison wrong; I'm AP smart.

"My mom doesn't want you here." Eric walks away from the front door toward the curb. I follow. He sits on the curb and motions for me to join him. "I'm worried about you, bro."

I sit down but quickly fall back on the grass, looking up the stars. "I'm fine."

"No, Just Man, you're not," Eric says, almost in a harsh teacher tone. "I heard about the thing with Jimmy at your stupid Seal fights. And all the trash you've been talking about him."

I can't think of anything to say to defend myself, so I count stars.

"It's one thing to kid around with me and Mychal but saying stuff like that about Jimmy and Anton to everyone? And the violence? What's up with that, Justin?"

"Anton came on to me," I say and then tell Eric how Anton came on to me after the party. Even telling it again gets me pretty worked up, especially since I need to share a locker room with Anton.

When I'm done, Eric says nothing for a long time. "So?"

"So? What kind of answer is that, Eric?"

"It sounds to me like he was trying to come *out* to you. Even if he was hitting on you, you couldn't just tell him you're not interested? You wouldn't beat up a girl for coming on to you."

I think about Allison. What I made her think I was going to do was even worse than hitting her. "No."

"So, maybe Anton came on to you, big deal. It doesn't mean anything. Let it go."

I sit up straight, like at attention. "I don't want people thinking I'm gay like him."

"Are you?" Eric asks. Odd how this isn't how Mychal reacted at all; he's still upset.

"No."

"Then it's over, but that still doesn't explain why you're acting so weird, does it?"

"No."

"Or why you want to stay here rather than at home. Just Man, what's up with your dad?"

Since Colonel Ladd hates Eric and the feeling is pretty much mutual, maybe it's safe. "Okay, I'm going to tell you something but if you tell another soul, I will choke you out."

"In your dreams," Eric says.

"My dad is—" I start, but I can't say the words. If I'm not in the house, if I don't speak to him, then I don't have to acknowledge it. Deny. Deny. Deny. "I think my dad is gay."

Eric laughs, not the reaction I want. I may choke him out anyway. "That's crazy."

"I know." He asks how I know, so I tell him what Calvin told me, but as we talk, I start putting pieces together: the stormy marriage to mom, no other girlfriends since their divorce, and this super close friendship with Colonel Parker. "So that's it. What do you think, Eric?"

Eric hems and haws, stops and starts like an old car engine. "What do you think?"

I spit it out: "I'm angry. But mostly confused. It changes everything."

"I don't see why, other than you'll have a lot more man smell in your house."

"Because I always wanted to be like him. You know that," I say, my voice cracking like a twelve-year-old. "It's like I had this vision of how my life would be, and it's all changed."

Eric stands up. I join him. "Just Man, have you talked with him about any of this?"

"No."

"I've been so jealous of the two of you since my dad split. You know what to do. Man up."

16

"Justin, is that you?" I hear a voice yell from the basement. It's three in the morning and he's downstairs. There's a clang of metal against metal.

For a second, I want to run, but I've got nowhere to go, no place I want to be. No future.

"I'll be up in a second," he calls. "We need to talk."

I look at the kitchen table. I remember another table, another talk—"*Your mother and I have arrived at the conclusion . . .*" Even something emotional, he rattled off in military speak. While we'd all shared a house between his deployments, we'd never been a real family. I'd always thought it was because he was married to the military, but I guess that was only half of it.

"No, I'll come down there." I shout that unfamiliar word "no" in his direction.

"Bring me a Gatorade from the fridge." I grab his drink and snag a Red Bull for myself. It's the middle of the night. I'm still running on fumes and fear. I need fuel.

Downstairs, he's on a bench doing curls with his right arm. "Thanks, Justin."

I hand him the drink. My hand shakes. I can tell he notices, but he says nothing. I set my drink on the floor next to me under the bars, and start doing pull-ups. He curls, I pull up. And we start to talk about nothing at all. Not about Jimmy. Or Allison. Or Colonel Parker.

It goes on that way for ten minutes. It's like football: you don't go full contact right away. You get in shape, run light practices and plays, and when you're ready, you start to hit. When he switches to curls with this left arm, I take to the bench to lift some serious weight.

With each lift, each groan, each bead of sweat, I feel like I'm getting closer to asking, to him answering, and to me knowing. He starts it. "Justin, just tell me something, anything."

Up goes the weight, down comes the truth. "Something Calvin said to me."

"Sure."

"He said the reason his dad is staying at Pearl is because he met someone."

Whoosh. Whoosh. Whoosh. Clang. Clang. Clang.

"Calvin said that someone was you."

I stop lifting, he stops curling, but he says nothing. My eyes stare at the ceiling.

"Dad, is that true?" I ask. The words heavier than all these weights combined.

I hear footsteps. Seconds later I see a shadow standing over me. "Yes."

And I wait for an apology for years of lying, but that one word is all he says, like I should accept it. Like it was an order.

"That's it?" I sit up, wipe the sweat away, and

stare up at him. "That's all you—"

"This changes nothing between us."

I fall back on the bench like he'd punched me between my eyes. "It changes everything."

"Justin, I don't see why." His tone is measured, unemotional, detached. Military discipline.

"Because all I've ever wanted is to be like you."

He steps closer. I feel a hand reaching out for me. "It changes nothing between us."

I sit back and try to raise my head to look at him, but the weight's too heavy. "I don't want to be like you. I don't want to be a disgusting freak."

The only thing louder than the silence minutes earlier is the sound of bone on bone as the back of his hand smacks me across the face for the first time I can remember. Before he can say another word or strike another blow, I sprint from the basement up the stairs. I grab the first set of keys I see and race toward the garage. The Harley's engine roars like thunder and I race away from my life, leaving a trail of blood, sweat, and tears in my wake.

07

"Where r u?" Eric texts. I rode up Tantalus, trying to get the courage to go over an edge, but like Colonel Ladd, I wasn't man enough to do the right thing. I got to school, slipped into the baseball field, and spent the morning sleeping in the dugout until Eric's call woke me up.

"School," I text back. "Call me."

Seconds later, Eric's on the phone. I recount the events in the basement. He doesn't say much. There's a lots of background noise, so I assume he's walking to school. "You okay?"

"He hit me hard," I say, "but I've taken harder shots from real men."

"Just Man, why are you talking that way?" Eric says. "My dad left us with nothing. He beat my mom and me. The only good thing he ever did was leaving. My dad wasn't a man. Your dad was always there for you, even when he was away. That's what a man does. What a man is. It doesn't matter if he's gay."

I hang up on Eric. After I take a whizz in the grass, I dial Mychal. "You with Eric?"

"No, your friend is whack," Mychal says. "I heard Anton's coming back to school today and I want to prank him, but Eric's not down with it. Sometimes I wonder about him."

"Eric's cool," I remind Mychal. "He's just a mama's boy, too sensitive, you know."

"I don't know why you stay friends with that fruit," Mychal counters. "Maybe we should prank him instead. All the hot girls think he's all that, so let's take him down a notch."

"I don't know. For a civilian, Eric's okay."

Mychal starts in on me, daring, goading. "You gonna man up or what, Justin?"

* * *

Eric's cold like Alaska to me in McFadden's class. I'm not sure if it's because I hung up on him or that I won't listen to him telling me I should be cool that my dad's gay. Mychal busts him a few times, but I don't join in the laughter at Eric's expense. It all seems wrong.

As luck or fate would have it, when Mychal and I meet up in the lunch line, Eric is chatting up Allison, who won't talk to me. So now it's like he's joined the enemy team. It makes this easier. Mychal and I pick up the big bowl of fruit and sprint toward Eric. We hurl it in his direction, but we're not quarterbacks so most of it misses him and lands on bystanders.

Eric says nothing but Allison screeches at me. Some people laugh, more people scream. Only one person blows a whistle. Coach Young. "Stewart and Ladd, in my office, now!"

He marches from the corner of the cafeteria toward the gym and his office. We follow as ordered. Mychal's cracking up, but just before we exit the cafeteria, I turn back and look at Eric. He's drenched in sticky fruit and juice, but he doesn't stink. That's me. That's me.

"Sit!" Coach Young says the second we're in his office. We obey. "What was that about?" Mychal says nothing. I follow his lead but I feel sick. "Nobody leaves here until I get an answer."

And I'm locked in another silent stalemate until Coach's phone rings. He takes the call. "They're in my office right now." Pause. "Don't worry, they will be disciplined." He hangs up.

Mychal sticks his long legs out in front of him, smiles, and finally speaks. "How many steps?" Like most coaches, Coach Young uses running the bleachers as punishment.

"It depends where you want to sit and watch your teammates. You're both off the team."

"For what? It was just a prank," Mychal says. "Fruit for a fruit. Pretty funny stuff."

Coach Young stands in front of us. "What is wrong with the two of you? You're supposed to be men. Sons of Seals. But you're little boys, afraid of anybody you think is different. You don't treat people like that. I would've thought your fathers taught you better."

"Please, Coach," Mychal whines, but I'm thinking of Dad's words to me: "Man up."

"And Justin, you doing something like this, knowing your father, it's shameful."

I don't ask Coach what "knowing your father" means. He knows about Dad. He doesn't care. Am I the only one who does?

18

"Justin, you can come in now," Coach says. He'd sent Mychal and me to the in-school suspension room until our fathers arrived. Mychal's dad got there first, so my wait is heavier. I got called when there's only a few minutes left in this day, my last on the Spartan football squad.

I walk back into the office. There's Coach, Colonel Ladd, and Colonel Parker.

"What's he doing here?" I point at Parker.

Before Colonel Ladd answers, Coach Young walks out the door and closes it behind him. Colonel Ladd motions for me to sit down, but I don't move a muscle.

"This is my fault," Colonel Ladd starts. Colonel Parker starts to say something, but Colonel Ladd talks right over him. "I should've made sure you understood the first time I tried to tell you."

Colonel Parker positions himself in front of the door. The office has no window so I'm as trapped as Jimmy was in our fights, and now I'm going to get the life choked out of me.

"I don't expect you to understand this, or even accept this, not today, maybe not tomorrow," Colonel Ladd says. "Maybe you'll never accept it, but the situation isn't changing."

"Your father and I . . ." Colonel Parker starts.

"I don't want to hear a word from you!" I shout. "This is your fault."

"Larry, please let me handle this," Colonel Ladd says softly, gently.

"Justin, look, this is who I am," he says. "It is how I've always been. I denied it for a long time because of how I was raised, because of the uniform, because I thought it was wrong."

"It is," I mumble.

"Being gay is no more being wrong than being left-handed, black, or having blue eyes," he explains. "It's how I was born, how I've always been. I just accept it now. I hope you will."

"I don't know." Another mumble, like my jaw, rather than Anton's, is broken.

"Justin, look, no matter what you think, I want you to know that I don't want this to change a thing between us. We've been through too much, too many miles, too much time apart, to have it all fall apart now. Those tough times should make you strong. You can handle this."

"I don't know," I repeat. "I don't know what to think."

"You don't need to think," he says. "This is family. You need to feel. How do you feel?"

I pause, look around the room. I glare at Parker, stare at Ladd, then say, "Betrayed."

They look at each other like they're trying to come up with something that would make me feel differently. "You're my son. I'm still your father."

"It was hard for Calvin," Colonel Parker adds. He's not helping.

"Justin, I can't tell you how you should or shouldn't feel about this, about anything," Colonel Ladd says. "But because I'm still your father I am going to tell you what you're going to do, so listen up."

As if by instinct, my head goes high and I stay still.

"First, you'll apologize to Eric. Second, you'll get a job so you can pay for replacing my windshield, and third, you're going to get your act together going forward, understand?"

I nod my heavy head.

"And here's what you're not going to do," he continues. "You're not going to bully Jimmy, Anton, or anybody else ever again because you think they're different. You went through that, so you should know better. You're not going to make any girls feel unsafe because it makes you feel manly. You're not going to retaliate in any way against Calvin for making clear what I couldn't."

Colonel Parker jumps in. "Or I'll put you in a sugar hold that will have you crying."

I stare at Colonel Ladd, my dad. He's right, he's right, he's right. But harder than any fight is admitting when you're wrong.

"Have I made myself clear?"

"Crystal."

"So we know where we stand. Are you going to keep acting like this or will you . . ."

"Man up," I finish his sentence. For the first time in a long time, Dad and I both smile.

ABOUT THE AUTHOR

Patrick Jones is the author of more than twenty novels for teens. He has also written two nonfiction books about combat sports, *The Main Event*, on professional wrestling, and *Ultimate Fighting*, on mixed martial arts. He has spoken to students at more than one hundred alternative schools, including residents of juvenile correctional facilities. Find him on the web at www.connectingya.com and on Twitter: @PatrickJonesYA.

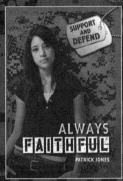

ALWAYS
FAITHFUL
PATRICK JONES

COLLATERAL
DAMAGE
PATRICK JONES / BRENT CHARTIER

COMBAT
ZONE
PATRICK JONES

FREEDOM
FLIGHT
PATRICK JONES

CHECK OUT ALL OF THE TITLES IN THE SUPPORT AND DEFEND SERIES